SWIM
SWIM
SINK

By Jenn Harney

Disney • HYPERION

Los Angeles   New York

First Edition, January 2020
1 3 5 7 9 10 8 6 4 2
FAC-020093-19340
Printed in Malaysia

This book is set in Burbank/House Industries; Minion Pro/Fontspring
Designed by Jenn Harney and Tyler Nevins
The illustrations were created digitally

Library of Congress Cataloging-in-Publication Data

Names: Harney, Jenn, author, illustrator.
Title: Swim swim sink / by Jenn Harney.
Description: First edition. • Los Angeles ; New York : Disney HYPERION, 2020.
  • Summary: "When one little duck keeps sinking, it relies on duckling
  ingenuity to stay afloat"— Provided by publisher.
Identifiers: LCCN 2018057033 • ISBN 9781368052764
Subjects: • CYAC: Stories in rhyme. • Ducks—Fiction. •
  Animals—Infancy—Fiction. • Floating bodies—Fiction.
Classification: LCC PZ8.3.H2182 Swi • DDC [E]—dc23
LC record available at https://lccn.loc.gov/2018057033

Reinforced binding
Visit www.DisneyBooks.com

For Rachel's
new oven

One happy duck sits down to rest.
Three tiny eggs. One twiggy nest.

Three eggs hatch.

Three tiny ducks.

Three tiny ducks in one straight line.

New, happy flock. All feeling fine.

Three tiny ducks jump right in.

SPLISH!

SPLISH! SPLASH!

Swim. Swim . . .

Sink.

Wait. What?

Let's try that again.

Three tiny ducks
jump right IN.

SPLISH! SPLISH! SPLASH!

Swim. Swim . . .

Sink.

Huh . . .
I didn't know
ducks *could* sink.
This is a problem.
Ducks need
to swim.

tap. tap.
tap.

AND all of this sinking is ruining the rhyme.

Or maybe not.

How about a push from below?

Water wings?

State-of-the-art scuba gear?

Three tiny ducks.
Swim. Swim. Float.
This clever duck
used its shell
as a BOAT.

Quack. **Quack.**